Lauren
the Puppy
Fairy

For Lauren Mary Shepherd,

my beautiful niece

Special thanks to

Narinder Dhami

ISBN-10: 0-545-04187-2
ISBN-13: 978-0-545-04187-4

20   17 18 19 20/0

Printed in the U.S.A.   40

First Scholastic printing, March 2008

Lauren
the Puppy
Fairy

by Daisy Meadows

SCHOLASTIC INC.

New York   Toronto   London   Auckland
Sydney   Mexico City   New Delhi   Hong Kong

The Fairyland Palace

Wetherbury Village

Strawberry Farm

The Spring Show

Bramble Stables

Jack Frost's Ice Castle

Jane Dillon's House

The Park

Kirsty's House

Jamie Cooper's House

The Wainwrights' House

Fairies with their pets I see
and yet no pet has chosen me!
So I will get some of my own
to share my perfect frosty home.

This spell I cast, its aim is clear:
to bring the magic pets straight here.
The Pet Fairies soon will see
their seven pets living with me!

Contents

Puppies on Show

"Look at that zucchini, Kirsty!" Rachel
Walker laughed, pointing at the giant
green vegetable on the display table. "It's
almost as big as I am!"

Kirsty Tate read the card propped in
front of the zucchini. "It won a prize,"
she announced. "It's the biggest vegetable
at the Wetherbury Spring Show!"

There were other enormous vegetables on the table. The girls stared at the giant-size carrots and onions. There were also huge bowls of daffodils, tulips, and bluebells. The best flower displays had won prizes, too.

"This is great!" Rachel declared. "I wish we had a Spring Show back home."

Rachel was staying in Wetherbury with Kirsty for the week, and the girls had spent the whole afternoon at the show. The field was crammed with booths selling homemade cakes, cookies, and jams, and there were pony rides and a huge red-and-yellow bouncy castle. Rachel and Kirsty were having a great time!

"I think we've been around the whole show," Kirsty said at last. "Mom and Dad will be here to pick us up soon."

"Should we take one last look at our favorite booth?" Rachel asked eagerly.

"You mean the one for the Wetherbury Animal Shelter?" Kirsty said with a smile.

Rachel nodded. "I want to see if they've found homes for those four puppies."

"I hope so," Kirsty said. "They were

really cute! And speaking of pets . . ." She lowered her voice so that she wouldn't be overheard. "Do you think we might find another fairy pet today?"

"We'll just have to keep our eyes open!" Rachel whispered in a determined voice.

No one else knew Kirsty's and Rachel's wonderful secret. They were friends with the fairies! Whenever there was trouble in Fairyland, the girls were always

happy to help. Mean Jack Frost caused
lots of problems for the fairies. This time,
he had stolen the seven Pet Fairies'
magical animals! But the mischievous pets
had escaped from Jack Frost, and were
now lost in the human world. Rachel and
Kirsty were trying to find the pets
and return them to their fairy owners
before Jack Frost's goblins caught them!

"It's too bad Jack Frost can't get his
own pet, instead of trying to steal
someone else's!" Kirsty remarked.

"Yes, but remember what the fairies
told us," Rachel reminded her. "In
Fairyland, the pets choose their
owners — and none of them has ever
chosen Jack Frost!"

"There must be the perfect pet for him
somewhere," Kirsty said thoughtfully.

"But it would have to be mean, just like him!"

The girls headed toward the animal shelter booth. But as they got closer Rachel's face fell. "Look, Kirsty," she said sadly. "There's still one puppy left."

Next to the booth was a large, fenced-in pen. When the girls had been there before, there had been four puppies in it — one brown, one white, and two black-and-white ones. Now only one black-and-white puppy remained. It was sitting in a corner, chewing on a piece of rope.

"Oh, poor pup!" Kirsty said, sighing. She bent over the pen. The puppy immediately dropped the rope and bounced over, its tail wagging furiously. "It looks lonely."

Mr. Gregory, the vet who ran the animal shelter, was taking down the posters pinned up on the booth. Kirsty smiled at him. She knew him because she'd taken her kitten, Pearl, to Mr. Gregory to get her shots.

"Hello," Mr. Gregory said, smiling back. "It's Kirsty Tate, isn't it? How's Pearl?"

Kirsty grinned. "She's great, thanks!" she replied. "What's the puppy's name, Mr. Gregory?"

"I call him Bouncer," the vet replied, "but it'll be up to his new owners to give him his real name."

The puppy was licking Kirsty's fingers through the wire fence. Bouncer looked so adorable that the girls just couldn't understand why no one had given him a home yet!

"Do you need any help packing up?"
Rachel asked Mr.
Gregory as he began
clearing pamphlets
from the table.

"That's very
kind of you,"
Mr. Gregory said
gratefully. "Would
you mind taking
Bouncer for a quick
walk around the grounds?
He's been cooped up in that pen
all day."

Rachel and Kirsty looked at each other
in excitement. "We'd love to!" they
chorused.

Mr. Gregory took a leash from his
pocket and opened the pen. Bouncer was

very excited when he saw the leash. He jumped around, giving little yaps of joy as the vet attached the leash to his collar.

"You walk him first," Rachel said to Kirsty. Kirsty took the leash and they set off, with the puppy running along beside them.

"Don't be too long, girls," Mr. Gregory called. "It'll only take me half an hour to pack up."

"OK," Rachel replied with a wave. Bouncer pulled excitedly at the leash, sniffing here and there, as the girls walked between the booths. Everyone else was starting to pack up, too. There were still a few children left on the bouncy castle, but their parents were doing their best to convince them to come down so that it could be deflated.

"I think Bouncer's going to pull off my arm!" Kirsty laughed as the puppy strained to go faster. "He's so excited."

"That's because he just spotted another dog," Rachel said, pointing ahead.

A brown-and-white puppy with a shaggy coat and long, floppy ears had seen them, too. It came bounding down the hill toward them.

"Isn't it cute?" Kirsty laughed as the pup drew nearer, waving its tail in greeting. "It's a springer spaniel, I think."

Bouncer was dancing around the girls' legs, bursting with excitement at the sight of his new puppy friend. The spaniel ran up to them, gave a little yap, and dashed off again.

Bouncer hurtled after it. Both girls' eyes widened in horror as they realized that the leash was now hanging loosely in Kirsty's hand. Somehow, Bouncer had gotten free!

"Oh, no!" Rachel gasped. "How did that happen?"

"I don't know," Kirsty replied anxiously. "But we'd better get him back right away!"

Puppy, Come Back!

Rachel and Kirsty dashed after the excited puppy.

"I'm sure the leash was attached to Bouncer's collar properly, Rachel," Kirsty panted. "There's something very strange going on here."

"You could be right," Rachel agreed as she caught up with the puppies.

The two dogs had stopped chasing
each other. Now they were running
around in circles, snapping playfully at
each other's tails.

Kirsty looked around. "At least they're
safe here," she pointed out. The puppies
were in a corner of the showgrounds, not
far from the high fence that separated the
field from the road. "They can't get out
onto the street."

"I wonder where the spaniel's owner is," Rachel said, sounding worried. "I don't see anyone nearby."

"I think there's a name tag on its collar," Kirsty said. She bent over the two puppies, which were rolling around on the grass. "Look, Rachel."

The girls stared closely at the spaniel's blue collar. A name tag in the shape of a little silver bone hung from it. SUNNY was written in glittering blue letters.

"Hello, Sunny," said Kirsty.

The spaniel licked Kirsty's hand and stared up at her with big brown eyes.

17

"There's no phone number or address," Rachel said, taking a closer look at the name tag.

"Let's tell Mr. Gregory when we take Bouncer back," Kirsty suggested. "He'll know what to do."

"Good idea," agreed Rachel.

Tail wagging, Sunny jumped to his feet and gave a happy little yap. But then, to Rachel and Kirsty's amazement, a sparkly, red rubber ball appeared in

midair and fell to the ground! The spaniel pounced on it and nudged it toward Bouncer.

"Did you see that, Kirsty?" Rachel gasped. "Or did I imagine it?"

"I saw a ball appear from thin air, if that's what you mean!" Kirsty replied, her voice shaking with excitement. The two dogs were playing with the ball now, knocking it back and forth. "Rachel, do you think Sunny could be one of the magic fairy pets?"

Rachel stared at the spaniel. He was standing with his head tilted to one side, watching Bouncer. "Yes, I think he might be," she agreed.

Bouncer dropped the ball to bark at Sunny. The ball landed on the grassy hill and began to roll away from the puppy, gathering speed. It was heading straight toward an open gate that led out onto the busy road. To the girls' horror, Bouncer suddenly turned and raced after it.

"Bouncer!" Rachel yelled as the puppy headed for the gate. "Kirsty, we have to stop him!"

With Sunny at their heels, the girls chased after the puppy, calling his name.

But Bouncer was too intent on catching
the ball to notice.

"We're too far away to catch him,"
Kirsty cried. "Bouncer, stop!"

But no sooner were the
words out of Kirsty's
mouth than Sunny
raced ahead of the
girls and gave
another little yap.
Rachel blinked as
she spotted a faint
shimmer of silver
fairy dust around
Sunny. The next
moment, a big, meaty bone
appeared in Bouncer's path.

The puppy skidded to a halt, ignoring
the ball as it bounced out of the gate and

onto the road. He was far more interested in the juicy bone! With a little yelp of delight, Bouncer lay down to have a good chew.

"That was close!" Kirsty panted, bending down to clip Bouncer's leash on again.

"Yes, that bone turned up just in time," Rachel agreed, patting Sunny. "You know, Kirsty, I think Bouncer getting off

his leash, and then the ball and the bone appearing out of nowhere, can only mean one thing . . ."

Kirsty nodded. "Sunny must be Lauren the Puppy Fairy's missing pet!" she declared.

Trouble Scoots Up

"He is!" laughed a light, silvery voice above the girls' heads.

Rachel and Kirsty glanced up. A pink balloon was floating down toward them. Holding onto the string, waving and smiling, was Lauren the Puppy Fairy.

"Hello," Kirsty and Rachel called, beaming happily. Sunny had spotted his owner, too, and was jumping around excitedly.

Lauren floated down toward them, her long light brown hair trailing in the breeze. She wore pink cargo pants, a cropped pink top, and sneakers. Waving her wand at the girls, she fluttered down to stand on Sunny's back.

"I'm so glad to see you, Sunny!" Lauren cried happily, dropping a tiny kiss on top of her pet's head. "And you too, girls."

"We're so glad you're here!" Kirsty replied.

"I think Sunny's tail is going to drop off if he doesn't stop wagging it so hard!" Rachel laughed.

The spaniel gave a happy bark, turning its shaggy head to look lovingly at its owner. Wondering what was going on, Bouncer looked up from his bone and trotted over to join them. He sniffed curiously at Lauren, and she put out her little hand to stroke his nose.

"I knew Sunny was around here somewhere," Lauren told the girls. "I'm so glad you found him!"

Rachel and Kirsty smiled.

"Actually, he found us!" Rachel said.

"Well, he found Bouncer," added Kirsty. "We've been lucky today, though. We haven't seen any goblins!"

"Yes, this was the easiest pet rescue so far," Rachel agreed.

"Ha, ha, ha!" The sound of cruel giggling behind them made Kirsty,

Rachel, Lauren, and even the puppies jump. Goblins! A shiny silver scooter was speeding along the path toward them. It was

crowded with goblins! Two of them were using their feet to push the scooter along as fast as they could. Three others were balanced on their shoulders, wobbling back and forth as the scooter zoomed along.

The girls and Lauren were taken by surprise! Before they could do anything, the scooter had crashed to a stop in front of them. The goblins tumbled off in a heap. One rolled toward Sunny, and another toward Bouncer.

"*Oof!*" Lauren gasped as the first goblin pushed her off Sunny's back, then snatched up the puppy.

"Is this the magic puppy?" the goblin yelled to the others.

"Don't know!" they shouted back, looking from Sunny to Bouncer. "Grab both!"

The first goblin leaped back on the scooter still clutching Sunny.

"Put him down!" Lauren yelled angrily, scrambling to her feet.

"Give him back!" shouted Rachel as the second goblin grabbed Bouncer, yanking the leash from Kirsty's hand, and then jumped onto the scooter.

"Catch us if you can!" jeered the goblins, whizzing away down the hill. The girls and Lauren watched as the scooter sped off, both puppies whimpering in fear.

"Jack Frost is going to be very pleased with us when he sees the magic puppy," one of the goblins shouted.

"Hooray!" cheered his goblin friends.

Grabbed by Goblins!

"We have to go after them!" Lauren declared, her face pale. "It will be quicker if I turn you into fairies, girls."

Kirsty and Rachel nodded. Hearts thumping, they waited as Lauren waved her wand and showered them with sparkling pink fairy dust. As soon as they were fairy-size, the girls fluttered up into the air to join their friend and chase down the goblins. But the goblins had a head start and were whizzing farther and farther away every second.

"They're getting away!" Rachel gasped.

The goblins were heading in the direction of the bouncy castle. Rachel, Kirsty, and Lauren could see that all the children had been cleared off the castle,  and it was slowly being deflated. Meanwhile, one of the goblins had climbed up onto the handlebars of the scooter and was yelling instructions at the others.

"Turn left! No, not that way," he roared furiously.

The other goblins weren't paying attention. They were struggling to hold the wriggling puppies and arguing loudly at the same time.

"Not that way — this way!"

"No, that's not right!"

One of the goblins grabbed the handlebars and tried to yank them in the opposite direction. The goblin who was perched there almost fell off! But the scooter still zoomed down the hill, pulling even farther away from Lauren, Rachel, and Kirsty.

"Faster, girls!" Lauren called. "We must stop them!"

Kirsty frowned. The goblins were so far ahead, it seemed almost impossible to catch up with them! Her gaze fell on the slowly deflating bouncy castle, and it gave her an idea. . . .

"Lauren!" Kirsty cried breathlessly. "Bouncer and Sunny are only puppies, but aren't the goblins scared of big dogs? I remember they were scared of Buttons, Rachel's dog."

Lauren nodded.

"Well, could you make a really big dog appear in front of the scooter?"

Kirsty went on. "Maybe we can force the goblins to swerve and crash into the bouncy castle. That would slow them down!"

"Great idea, Kirsty!" Rachel said eagerly. Lauren was already lifting her wand.

As the girls watched, a shower of glittery pink sparkles whooshed from the tip of Lauren's wand toward the goblins. There was a puff of pink smoke, and just to the left of the scooter, a German shepherd appeared out of thin air. Rachel and Kirsty stared at it in surprise. This was no ordinary German shepherd. It was black with white stripes, just like a zebra!

Woof! Woof! Woof! the dog barked loudly.

The goblins screeched with fear.

"A big, scary dog!" the one sitting
on the handlebars yelled. "Quick,
get away!"

All the goblins grabbed the handlebars
and wrenched them to the right.
Immediately, the scooter careened away
from the dog, straight toward the
bouncy castle.

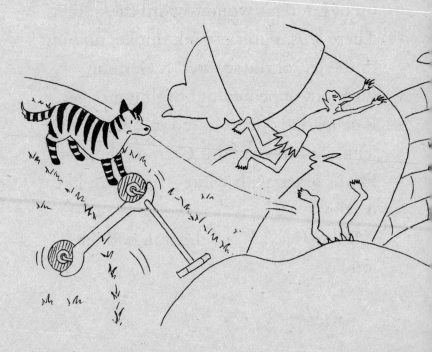

"No!" shouted the goblin on the handlebars. "We're going to crash!"

But he was too late. As Lauren, Rachel, and Kirsty watched, the scooter hit the bouncy castle. The goblins went flying! The puppies barked and the goblins shrieked with anger, but they all landed safely on the castle, disappearing into its folds.

Quickly, Lauren waved her wand to make the German shepherd disappear. Then she, Rachel, and Kirsty flew over to the bouncy castle.

"It's a good thing there's hardly anyone around!" Kirsty said, looking relieved.

"Yes, but what about the man who's packing up the bouncy castle?" Rachel asked. "He's sure to come back soon. How are we going to get the puppies and the goblins out of there?"

New Friends

Lauren, Kirsty, and Rachel hovered over
the bouncy castle, wondering what to do.
Then, to their relief, they suddenly heard
a tiny bark.

A moment later, Sunny's head popped
up. He wriggled out of the castle, barking
with delight as soon as he spotted Lauren.
Bouncer followed him, and together they

bounced toward the edge of the half-deflated castle, enjoying this new game.

"Sunny!" Lauren called, holding her arms open.

Rachel and Kirsty saw a shimmer of glittering magic around the spaniel as it shrank to fairy-pet size. Then he jumped off the bouncy castle and bounded magically through the air toward Lauren.

"It's OK, Bouncer," laughed Rachel, seeing the puppy stare at Sunny in surprise. "It's fairy magic!"

"Don't you try it, though!" Kirsty added with a laugh.

Sunny had run straight into Lauren's arms and was now licking her nose gently. Laughing, Lauren raised her wand. In three sparkling seconds, Rachel and Kirsty were back to their normal size.

Bouncer blinked. Then he jumped
down from the castle and dashed joyfully
over to Rachel and Kirsty. Rachel
picked up his leash and held it tightly as
she bent down to pet him.

"What's Bouncer looking at?" asked
Kirsty, noticing that the little puppy
was peering curiously at something
behind them.

Rachel turned to see. "Here comes the bouncy castle man!" she whispered. "Lauren — you and Sunny had better hide!"

Lauren nodded. Still holding Sunny, she zoomed down to hide in Rachel's pocket.

The bouncy castle operator was a young man with a friendly face. He smiled at Kirsty and Rachel. "Hi," he said. "Did you enjoy the Spring Show?"

"It was great," Kirsty replied, and Rachel nodded.

The castle operator glanced down at Bouncer, who was sniffing eagerly at the man's legs.

"What a cute puppy!" he said,

bending down to scratch Bouncer's head. "My daughter, Annie, would love a dog like this."

"How old is Annie?" asked Rachel.

"She'll be six next week," the man replied. "Actually, her mom and I are planning on getting her a puppy for her birthday. Excuse me," he went on, "I have to get this castle put away."

Whistling to himself, the man went around the back of the bouncy castle, where all the cables were hidden. "What are we going to do?" Rachel whispered as Lauren and Sunny popped their heads out of her pocket. "He's not going to be very happy when he finds a bunch of angry goblins in his castle!"

But Kirsty was shaking her head and laughing. "Look!" She pointed at the front of the castle. "He won't see them, because they're coming out on this side. And it's the goblins who don't look very happy!"

The goblins were finally emerging from beneath the folds of rubber. They were

grumbling and groaning and blaming
one another, as usual. Two of them were
dragging the silver scooter along.
Complaining loudly, they all jumped to
the ground and stalked off, pulling the
scooter behind them.

"That was all your fault!"

"I told you we were going to crash!"

"And now we've lost the magic puppy. Who's going to tell Jack Frost?"

Kirsty, Rachel, and Lauren couldn't help laughing.

"Daddy! Daddy, where are you?" came a voice.

Immediately, Lauren ducked out of sight, and the girls turned to see who was coming.

A girl with dark curly hair and big blue eyes was running toward them. "Daddy, where are you?" she called again.

"Around the back of the castle, sweetheart," the man yelled back.

"That must be Annie," Kirsty whispered.

Just then, Annie caught sight of Bouncer. Her face broke into a huge smile, and she dashed straight toward him. "What a sweet puppy!" she said, kneeling down to hug him. Bouncer yapped a greeting and  licked her cheek, his tail wagging furiously.

"Oh, I wish I had a puppy like you!" Annie said to Bouncer.

"Would you like to hold his leash?" Rachel asked, offering it to her.

Annie's eyes lit up. "Can I really?" she gasped. "Oh, thank you!"

She took the leash, and the girls watched as Annie led Bouncer on a little walk in front of the castle. Bouncer bounded alongside her, clearly enjoying himself. Then he spied the untied shoelace of one of Annie's sneakers and pounced on it, grabbing it in his teeth.

Annie laughed and crouched down to tug the lace gently. Kirsty and Rachel smiled as Bouncer held on to it, enjoying the game.

Suddenly, Kirsty nudged Rachel. "Look, Rachel!" she whispered, her voice full of excitement. "There's a magical sparkle all around Annie and Bouncer!"

Puppy Love

Rachel stared at the little girl and the puppy. Kirsty was right! A shimmery haze hung in the air around them.

"Fairy magic!" Rachel whispered back. "Bouncer's meant to be with Annie. She's the owner he's been waiting for!"

At that moment, the man came out from behind the bouncy castle, which was now almost fully deflated. He smiled when he saw Annie and Bouncer playing together.

"That's really a great puppy, girls," he said with a smile. "Which one of you is the owner?"

Rachel saw her chance. "The puppy's  not mine or Kirsty's," she explained. "It's from the animal shelter booth. Its brothers and sisters have all been adopted today, and it's the only one left."

"Oh, really?" The man frowned. "I didn't see the animal shelter booth."

Annie had been listening to their conversation, her eyes wide. Now she

tugged at her dad's sleeve. "Daddy!"
she cried. "This poor little
puppy doesn't have
a home!"

Rachel and Kirsty
held their breath as
they waited for
Annie's dad to reply.
He looked at the
eager face of his little
girl and then down into
Bouncer's brown eyes.

"Well . . ." he began, "I'll finish up
here, and then we'll go over to the
animal shelter booth. But don't get your
hopes up too much, Annie. Someone else
may want to adopt that dog."

"Oh, thank you, Daddy!" Annie
gasped joyfully, throwing her arms

around him. Rachel and Kirsty beamed
at each other. Even Bouncer seemed to
know that something exciting was going
on, because he gave two happy barks.

The man disappeared behind the castle
to finish his work, and Annie and
Bouncer went with him.

"Good job, girls!" Lauren said, flying
out of Rachel's pocket.
Sunny followed her,
bounding through the
air to perch on Kirsty's
shoulder. "Annie is the
puppy's perfect owner!"

"Everything's worked
out wonderfully," Rachel
said, and Kirsty nodded.

"I don't know how I can ever thank
you," Lauren went on gratefully.

"Without you, I wouldn't have gotten Sunny back."

"*Woof!*" Sunny agreed, rubbing his tiny black nose against Kirsty's cheek.

"But we have to go home to Fairyland now," Lauren said, raising her wand. "Everyone will be anxious to find out if I've gotten my magic pet back. Say good-bye, Sunny."

Sunny gave a little yap, wagging his tail so hard it tickled Kirsty's ear. Then he ran over to Lauren, who waved her wand. A shower of sparkling fairy dust fell around them.

"Oh!" Lauren called, "I almost forgot! Say good-bye to Barney for me!"

Confused, Rachel and Kirsty looked at each other.

"Who's Barney?" asked Rachel. But Lauren and Sunny had vanished in a haze of glittering magic.

A moment later, Annie, Bouncer, and Annie's dad walked up.

"Daddy, we'll have to give my new puppy a name," Annie was saying. "Can I call him Barney?"

Her dad smiled. "We need to talk to the people at the animal shelter before we make any plans," he said. "But if it's OK for us to adopt him, then we'll call him Barney."

Rachel and Kirsty grinned at each other as they followed Annie and her father toward the animal shelter booth.

"So *that's* why Lauren told us to say good-bye to Barney!" Kirsty whispered. "Mr. Gregory's going to be really happy that Barney's found a home at last."

The two girls beamed as they watched Annie's father chatting to Mr. Gregory. The vet was nodding and smiling, while Annie and Barney were chasing each other across the grass.

"Everyone in Fairyland is going to be happy that Sunny's safely home again, too!" Rachel added.

Kirsty nodded. "I love happy endings!" she said, sighing.

Lauren the Puppy Fairy has her pet
back. Now can Rachel and Kirsty help

Harriet
the Hamster
Fairy?

Hamster-sitting

"Here we go," Kirsty Tate said to her best friend, Rachel Walker, turning the key in the back door of her neighbors' house. "Nibbles! Time for breakfast!" she called as the door swung open. "Just wait until you see him," she said to Rachel with a grin. "He's adorable. I love hamster-sitting!"

Kirsty's neighbor, Jamie Cooper, had asked Kirsty to feed Nibbles, his little orange-and-white hamster. He and his parents were away. She had said yes immediately!

"We just need to give him food and water," Kirsty told Rachel. "And if we're lucky, he might eat sunflower seeds out of our hands!"

"How sweet!" Rachel said. "Where's his cage?"

"Over here," Kirsty replied, heading into the living room.

An excited feeling bubbled up inside Rachel as she followed her friend. They were going to see another pet after all. Over the last few days, she and Kirsty had had some very exciting pet adventures!

Kirsty led Rachel across the living room to the table where Nibbles's cage stood. But when the girls arrived, the saw that something was wrong. The cage door was wide open!

"Oh, no!" Kirsty cried. "Don't tell me that Nibbles managed to escape on the very first day I'm looking after him!" She carefully put her hand into the cage and searched through the wood shavings and newspaper shreds for the little hamster, but it was too late. The cage was empty.

THE WEATHER FAIRIES

Rain or Shine, It's Fairy Time!

RAINBOW magic™

There's Magic in Every Series!

The Rainbow Fairies

The Weather Fairies

The Jewel Fairies

The Pet Fairies

The Fun Day Fairies

The Petal Fairies

The Dance Fairies

Read them all!

■ SCHOLASTIC

www.scholastic.com

www.rainbowmagiconline.com

HiT entertainment

RMFAIRY

SPECIAL EDITION

Three Books in One!
More Rainbow Magic Fun!